FAERIE

Written and Illustrated by Jody Bergsma

GALLERY PRESS

PUBLISHING, INC.

GALLERY PRESS

PUBLISHING, INC.

1344 King St ❀ Bellingham WA 98226
Phone: (360) 733-1101 ❀ (800) BERGSMA ❀ Fax: (360) 647-2758
bergsma@bergsma.com ❀ **www.bergsma.com**

Library of Congress Control Number: 2002100911
ISBN number: 0-9717117-0-4

Summary: The faerie queen of Nagala sends her subjects to Lugin to avert a growing disaster through an encounter with the queen of goblins.

1. Faeries 2. Children's fiction 3. Wizard 4. Goblins

36pp. and 23_ x 28_ cm cover size

Original illustrations and artwork entirely by Jody Lynn Bergsma. Story by Jody Lynn Bergsma.

Illustrations are Winsor & Newton™ artist watercolor on Arches™ watercolor paper.

Published in the United States
Printed in Seoul, Korea by Book & Stationery International Company
Book Design: Molly Murrah, Murrah & Company, Kirkland, WA

Dedication

To my Irish grandmother, Dorothy Lilly Knight,
and to her daughter, my mother, Arden Nellie Knight,
who taught me there is more to life than meets the eye
...and that love changes things.

Special Thanks

To my editor and mentor, Antoinette Botsford, for her splendid help
in the writing of *Faerie*. I will never forget our meeting at the waterfall
where our discussion led to the birth of this story.

To Gail Smedley for her brilliant mind and help with the final edit.

To Sheila Goodwin and Francesca Tolchin for their insight
into the story and their loving friendship.

To Jessica Bergsma & Daniele O'Connell for long and dedicated hours of typing.

All was not well in Nagala, land of elves and faeries.

Lightning flashed behind an angry sky while dry, electric winds charged the air. Pacing inside the castle garden, Rhiannon, Queen of Faerie, awaited news from her winged messengers. Hearing fluttering overhead, the queen looked up to see Falana, the blue faerie. "Beloved Queen!" Falana cried, "We can't find our Gryphon anywhere." Ruby, the red faerie, and Tara, the green faerie, alighted beside her.

Queen Rhiannon's eyes darkened.
"I fear Gryphon has been captured in Lugin.
Now I must send you to rescue him."

"How can we leave our kingdom?" the faeries wailed. "How can
we leave you?"

"You are faeries of the rainbow. Your light is stronger than the
darkest shadow."

The queen called for Skyla, the unicorn, and said, "Skyla will take you where you need to go. Stay together. Goblins have invaded Lugin, and you will need each other."

The faeries trembled.

Taking a key from her pocket, the queen gave it to Ruby. "This will open many locks. Guard it well." Then she gave each faerie a colored wand. "In time you will learn the special magic of these wands." Opening a hidden door in an ancient oak, Rhiannon pointed the way to Lugin.

As the faeries and Skyla proceeded through the entrance, they heard Rhiannon's last fading words: "In nature you will hear my voice."

After ascending a long dusty stairway, they came to a locked door. Ruby inserted the key and the door creaked open.

"Cobwebs everywhere!" whispered Tara.

"Bats!" cried Ruby. In fright, she turned and tripped, dropping the key. A bat seized it and flew away squeaking triumphantly.

"After them!" shouted Falana, leaping into the air. But Tara, Ruby, and Skyla were trapped in a tangle of cobwebs and could not follow.

Flying after the bats, Falana saw a boy reach to receive the jeweled key.

The faerie lunged for the key, tackling the boy who in return grabbed the squirming faerie.

"Who are you?" he demanded.

"I'm Falana, head of the rainbow faeries, and you have my key," she panted, struggling to escape his grasp. "Who are you?"

"I am the wizard, Kevin. I serve the queen of Lugin and am in search of her stolen jewels. I asked my friends the bats to bring me any they could find. Tell me what a rainbow faerie is doing in Lugin."

After Falana finished her story, Kevin said, "This is very strange. Gryphon has disappeared and so has my dragon. Together we must regain what has been lost."

Hoping to find Tara, Ruby, and Skyla, they returned to the great tangle of cobwebs. Alas, no one was there.

Kevin pointed to something glittering on the ground.

"Unicorn dust!" Falana exclaimed. "Skyla left us a trail."

They followed the luminous powder through the enchanted forest of Lugin to a rocky, dry land. As the colors in the landscape faded, so did their magic.

Falana's wings slowly disappeared and Kevin said, "Your special powers will grow weak in the barren world that awaits us. We now must travel by night when monsters are sleeping, for we have come to the edge of Goblin Land where no good thing abides."

While the blue faerie chased the bats, Ruby and
Tara untangled themselves and Skyla from the cobwebs.
Searching for Falana, they rode unknowingly toward
Goblin Land. As they neared its rocky borders, their
wings began to shrink and Skyla's horn to vanish. They
soon looked like two ordinary girls riding a white pony.

Tara blinked hard, trying not to cry. "No wings..."

"...and we're lost," sniffled Ruby.

The hornless unicorn took them down a well-worn
path. Nearby, the sound of rushing water grew louder as
they came to a stone bridge.

"Well, what have we here?" snarled a troll. "Two little girls and a pony! What a treat!"

Skyla shivered beneath the faeries. Ruby and Tara noticed that the troll's eyes did not smile.

Ruby took a deep breath. "We're looking for bats. Have you seen any?"

"Yesss, I've seen bats! Just cross me bridge," the troll crooned with a moist smile.

As Skyla stepped onto the bridge, other trolls popped out and threw a huge net over the screaming faeries. "Got 'em!" yelled another troll. "Heh heh! We can turn 'em inta troll girls wit' a wee bit o' troll juice."

Binding Ruby and Tara to Skyla, the trolls marched them deeper into the mountains where huge goblins prodded the travelers with their spears. "Hurry along now or we'll hafta eat ya, " they sneered.

Forced to follow the goblins through a dark and narrow maze, the faeries grew more confused at every turn. Finally, they reached a stone castle where monster statues and dim lanterns lined the halls. Even the noisy trolls grew silent in the gloom.

A disgusting odor wafted through the cavern.

"What is that?" hissed Ruby. "It smells like stinky feet."

"Silence!" barked the guard. "Dis here da chamber of Woldy, Queen of Goblins!" Down a long aisle they saw the queen snorting and grunting over a platter of boiled toads.

"There's the smell," whispered Ruby.

"She could use some table manners..." Tara muttered.

"...and look at her hair!" Ruby gasped.

The goblin queen pushed her matted hair aside and peered at them. "Useless l'il girls an' a pony," she squawked. "Didja bring me anything? Some jewels, perhaps?"

Tara blurted out, "My friend here, her name is Ruby..."

"...and her name is Emerald," added Ruby, cleverly.

"Perfect, and somethin' I don't have already... two livin' gems. You an' your pony will care fer our prisoners. Now, off wit' ye!" screeched the hag.

Deep in the mountains, Kevin and Falana were still following Skyla's shimmering trail. Tiptoeing past the sleeping goblins, they reached the castle maze. Kevin read the sign at the gate:

All ye who come here, now beware,
of yonder kingdom, goblins' lair.
Death to all who enter in,
without a guide the maze will win.

Kevin shuddered, "In this loveless world the unicorn trail is fading and we may never find our way through the maze."

Falana sighed, "If only Rhiannon were here."

At the sound of the faerie queen's name, spiders rushed from the crevices and filled the path. "Follow our thread through the ma-aze, we-eze come to help you," they whispered.

The spiders led them through dark secret halls to a closed door. "Us-s-se yoo-ur ke-ey," they hissed. A lonely shaft of light cut through the darkness as Kevin turned the key in the lock.

The door opened silently. Falana and Kevin found themselves on a ledge overlooking the queen's guards. Voices rose in dreadful song as the goblins danced around their queen.

Dragon's tail, blood of cat,
wings of faerie, gryphon, bat,
then last we'll add a unicorn,
three faeries and we'll be reborn!

"Eat them all! Eat them all!" howled the queen.

In horror Falana cried out. As Kevin lunged towards her to cover her mouth, he lost his footing and tumbled all the way to the warty feet of Queen Woldy.

Terrified, Falana ran.

In a far corner of the castle, a goblin prodded Ruby and Tara towards a dungeon full of captured prisoners. "Off ta werk wit' ye," he snapped. "Here's pails and mops ta clean da cages. You'll find water in da well in da courtyard."

"L-look. There's Gryphon!" stuttered Tara.

"And a dragon!" gasped Ruby.

When a cat meowed, the guard whacked it with a stick.

"Dis last empty cage will soon be full, and den da light will go out in all of Nagala, and Queen Rhiannon will be no more!" growled the goblin guard. His ghoulish laughter filled the dungeon as he hobbled away.

The faeries eye's widened as they read the sign on the cage:

"Reserved for three Faeries and a Unicorn"

Falana ran through the darkened halls using her hands for eyes. A bat squealed, "Follow, follow!" The helpful creature led her to a courtyard where, feeling hopeless and exhausted, the faerie began to cry.

Something gently touched her hand. "Over there, over there," squeaked a mouse.

Through her tears Falana saw what looked like two little girls. "Could it be?" she wondered. "It is! It's Ruby and Tara!"

Overjoyed, she hurried toward her friends. They greeted each other with squeals of delight.

When Ruby and Tara told Falana of the sign on the cage and the goblins' plot, she sighed, "There's still hope. Now that we're wingless, they won't know we're faeries. Let's hide by this old tree until dark when the goblins fall asleep. Then we'll find a way to save Kevin and the others."

Huddled under the tree by the well, the faeries and Skyla heard a strange murmuring. "Listen," whispered Tara.

The rustling wind sang, "Co-o-omb her hair."

The bubbling water gurgled, "Wa-a-sh her feeet."

And the murmuring tree sighed, "Light a fire with my dry br-raanches to keep her warm."

The faeries recognized Rhiannon's voice in the sounds of nature and knew what to do.

After his fall, Kevin lay sprawled at the foot of the goblin queen's throne.

"A wizz-zard," snarled the hag. "Jus' what a queen needs. And what a pretty little wand." The queen pinched Kevin's arm. "Hee hee hee! Youz is a bit young, but youz will do."

A lump of fear grew in Kevin's throat as the goblins chained his neck.

When night fell, Queen Woldy retired to her chamber, dragging the chained boy behind her. The goblin queen commanded, "Sing to me, wizz-zard, sing me to sleep."

Gathering his courage, Kevin began his favorite lullaby.

The queen yawned, her eyes drooped, and she fell fast asleep.

As Kevin sang, the friendly bat led Falana and the others to the snoring queen's chamber.

At the sight of Falana, Kevin's eyes shone in relief. The faeries whispered what they'd heard from Queen Rhiannon.

"Comb her hair?" sputtered the boy. "She'll never let me do that."

"You must try," pleaded Falana, "after all you are the wizard."

Kevin crept closer to Queen Woldy. Saying a magical verse, he gently pried his wand from her bony fingers. "**Hoona poona ala loona,**" and through the wave of sparkling sound, the wand transformed into a comb.

The goblin queen awoke and demanded, "What's that ugly thing fer?"

Kevin replied, "You may find it ugly now, but soon it will glimmer with gems of every color when I have used it for its true purpose."

"And what might that be?" asked the suspicious crone.

"It must be used to comb the hair of the great ruler: **She Who Must Be Obeyed.** Do you know where I might find her?"

"Oh, yes. Tis me," puffed the queen. "Does me get to keep it then?"

"Why not?" shrugged Kevin.

"Well then, me who must be obeyed commands you to comb me hair."

Kevin began to undo a lifetime of snarls. "Oh, very nice, yes," sniffed the old goblin. "No one has ever combed me hair before, not even me own m-mother."

As the boy tenderly combed her hair, tears fell from Queen Woldy's eyes. When at last her hair flowed smoothly down her back, Kevin washed the queen's feet with her own hot tears.

Between shuddering breaths, the queen sobbed, "No one h-has ever w-washed me feet b-before, not even m-me own m-mother."

Soon, her feet gleamed with the pinkest, softest skin. She began to shiver.

"Are you cold, Majesty?" asked Kevin, wrapping a shawl around her shoulders.

"Yes, cold, very cold," she replied. And Kevin lit a fire to keep her warm.

"No one has ever built me a fire before," sniffled the queen. "Me own goblin mother was made of stone, and what does a stone care if it is cold?"

The faeries and Skyla came out from behind the curtain to see
more clearly, and as they watched Woldy's hardened face change,
something changed in them as well. Skyla's horn was reappearing
as were the faeries' wings!

The goblin guards were waking in the morning light and one
of them shouted, "Look! They be faeries! Grab 'em!"

"Quick, we must complete the transformation!" shouted Kevin."
Take out your wands and point them at Skyla!"

The faeries circled Skyla while the wizard proclaimed:

By the colors of three faeries
who together make one light,
we command you to transform,
that this land may be reborn.

Red, green, and blue beams flashed from the faeries' wands. Color swirled around the unicorn until a fountain of light burst from her horn. Zigzagging through the room, the light touched the queen and she fell to the ground.

A deep rumbling engulfed the castle.

Cracks slashed the faces of the statues lining the halls. Crates and boxes toppled freeing stolen treasure and like a million rainbow butterflies, light and color flooded the land.

Kevin's chain dropped from his neck, the doors on the cages flew open, and the prisoners sprang free. They rushed into the open courtyard seeking refuge under the old tree, where they watched the castle tumble to the ground.

In the settling dust the oak tree began to shimmer, and a door opened in its trunk revealing Queen Rhiannon. As she climbed the enchanted stairs towards them, Rhiannon said, "You have achieved what I believed you could. For it is known that when the light grows stronger, the darkness dims."

They turned toward the ruins of the goblin palace and saw a female form rising from the rubble.

"That is my twin sister, Anawold," confessed Rhiannon. "The goblins stole her when she was young, gave her to a stone mother, and made me powerless to save her."

"Only the kind heart of a wizard and the courage of three faeries could break their evil spell. Anawold does not yet know who she is, but she will learn," and with love in her eyes, Rhiannon walked toward the transformed goblin queen.

The End

We honor the place that is not light,
the forest in winter, the cold and night.
Yet know that spring and summer will come,
and with the dawn will rise the sun.

JODY LYNN BERGSMA
Author / Illustrator

FAERIE is the third book written and illustrated by Jody Bergsma and is the third book in the **DragonFire** series. An internationally acclaimed watercolor artist, Jody owns and operates the Bergsma Gallery in Bellingham, Washington. Jody's gallery features a wonderful café and has a warehouse facility close by, which ships her products to thousands of store locations worldwide.

Jody is best known for two diverse art styles. **Dream Keepers**, consists of wide-eyed characters and whimsical creatures that celebrate family, friendship, and love with inspirational sayings and assurance that dreams do come true. Her second style, **Natural Elements**, includes symbolism and scenes of the nature and wildlife that surround her.

Jody has recently completed special artistic projects for Sea World, Busch Gardens, Universal Studios, and the National Aquarium in Baltimore. She invites new and long time collectors to visit her gallery in Bellingham where her limited edition prints, art cards, and other gift items are sold.

For further information on Jody and to see her travel schedule, please go to the company Web site at **www.bergsma.com**, or write to her at the following address:

Bergsma Gallery / Gallery Press Publishing, Inc.
1344 King St. ❖ Bellingham, WA 98226 ❖ (800) BERGSMA
www.bergsma.com

JODY BERGSMA CHILDRENS BOOKS ❖ AWARDS & HONORS

DREAMBIRDS
By David Ogden, illustrated by Jody Bergsma

Winner – Best Children's Book
Coalition of Visionary Retailers, 1998

A native boy searches for his elusive dream bird and its powerful gift.

SKY CASTLE
By Sandra Hanken, illustrated by Jody Bergsma

Winner – Children's Choice Award
Children's Book Council, 1999
Winner – Silver Medal Best New Voice
Benjamin Franklin, 1999
Winner – Best Editing
Northwest Association of Book Publishers
Finalist – Best Book
Northwest Association of Book Publishers

Alive with fairies, parrots, dolphins and talking lions, this magical tale inspires us to believe in the power of our dreams.

THE RIGHT TOUCH
By Sandy Kleven, LCSW, illustrated by Jody Bergsma

Winner – Gold Medal Best Parenting Book
Benjamin Franklin, 1999
Selected as outstanding by the Parents Council, 1998
Finalist – Small Press Award, 1998

This beautifully illustrated read-aloud story teaches children how to prevent and/or deal with sexual abuse.

DRAGON
Written and illustrated by Jody Bergsma

Winner – Best Children's Book Award
Coalition of Visionary Retailers, 2000
Finalist – Children's Book of the Year
ForeWord Magazine, 2000

Born on the same day, a gentle prince and a fire-breathing dragon share a common destiny. This is the first book in the DragonFire series.

THE LITTLE WIZARD
Written and illustrated by Jody Bergsma

Winner – Best Children's Book
Coalition of Visionary Retailers, 2001
Winner – Best Color Cover
Northwest Association of Book Publishers, 2001
Third Place – Children's Book of the Year
ForeWord Magazine, 2001
One of Three Finalists – Book of the Year
Northwest Association of Book Publishers, 2001
Winner – Best Cover
Benjamin Franklin Award, 2001

A young boy undertakes a perilous quest to save his mother's life. Powerful illustrations weave a mystical spirit throughout this exquisite story. This is the second book in the DragonFire series.

All of the above books have been designed by Molly Murrah, Murrah & Company, Kirkland, WA.